Follow
the Line
through the house

words and art by

Laura
Ljungkvist

VIKING

Follow the line and go inside.
Look around. What can you find?

Search and peek,
discover, explore.

There is so much to see
behind each door.

Welcome to the house!

Turn the page and step into . . .

the kitchen.

Turn the page to choose
a snack from . . .

the refrigerator.

How many pickles are in the jar?

Which foods are green?

What would you use to make a sandwich?

What shape is the Swiss cheese?

What would you choose for a snack?

Can you find the cherries that fell out of the bag?

Now go downstairs and explore the basement.

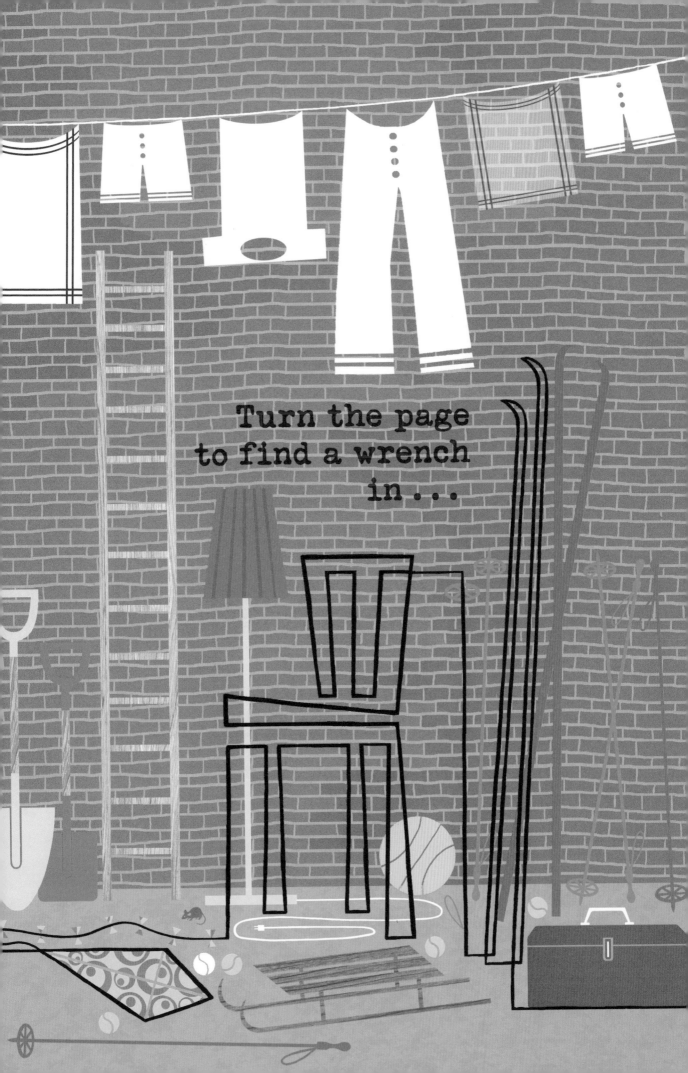

Turn the page
to find a wrench
in . . .

the toolbox.

How many saws can you count?

Which tools have wooden handles?

What would you use to hammer a nail?

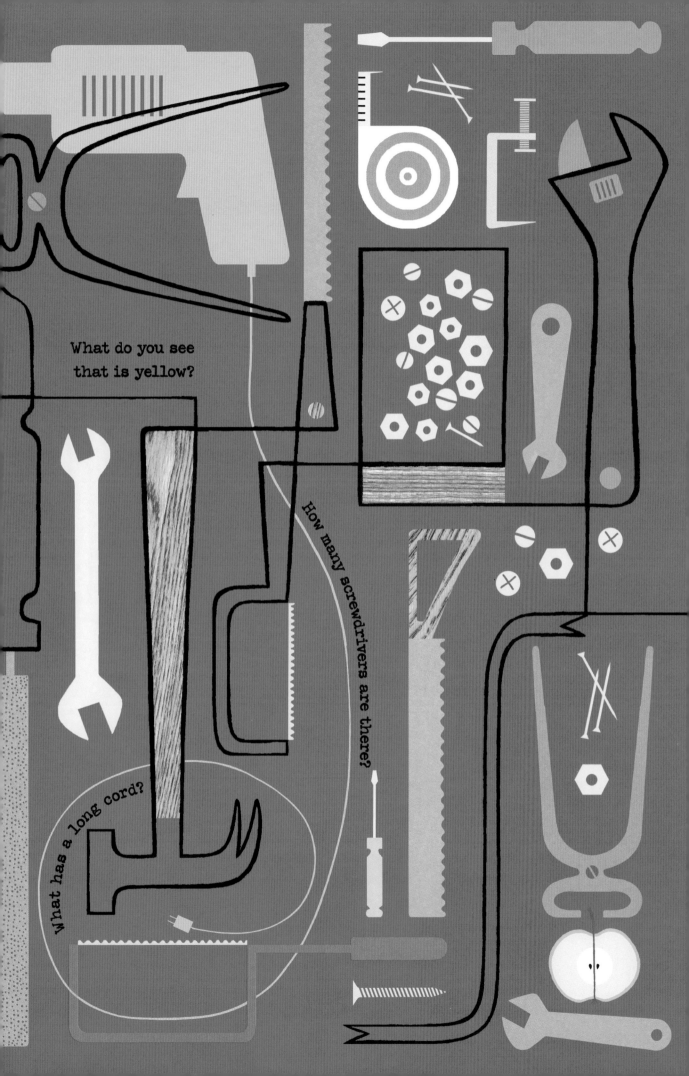

What do you see
that is yellow?

How many screwdrivers are there?

What has a long cord?

Let's go upstairs
to the master bedroom.

Turn the page and play
dress-up in...

the big closet.

How many bow ties can you count?

What would you wear to the beach?

Which shirts are striped?

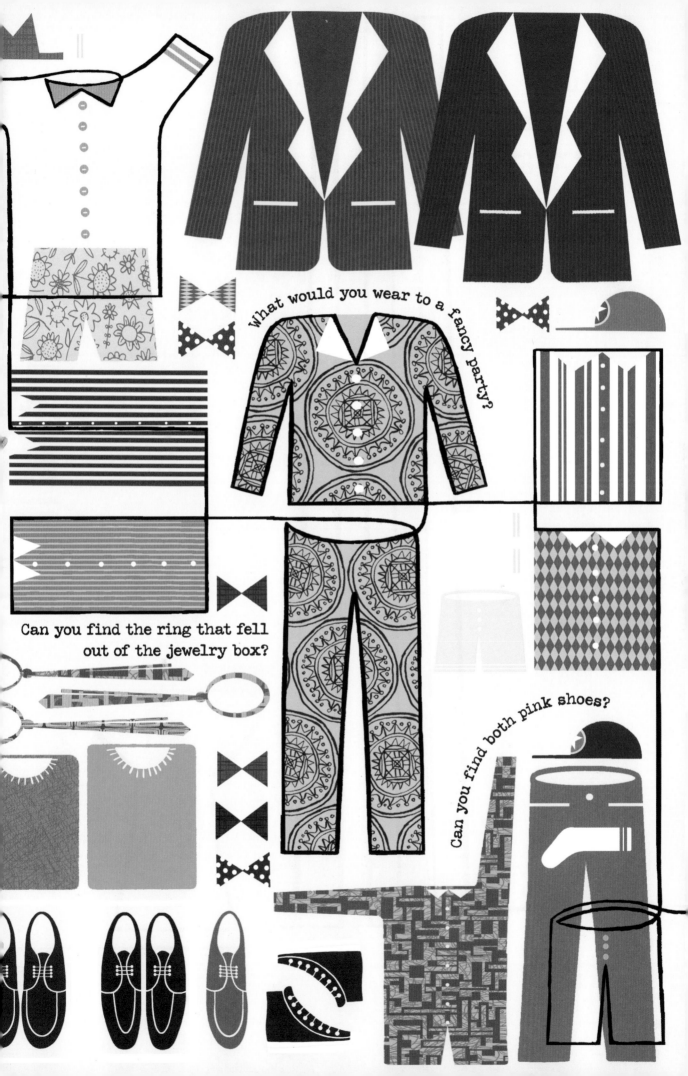

What would you wear to a fancy party?

Can you find the ring that fell out of the jewelry box?

Can you find both pink shoes?

The
bathroom
is right
next
to the
bedroom.

Turn the page to peek into . . .

the cabinet.

What color is the electric razor?

How many bottles of nail polish are there?

What would you use to clean your teeth?

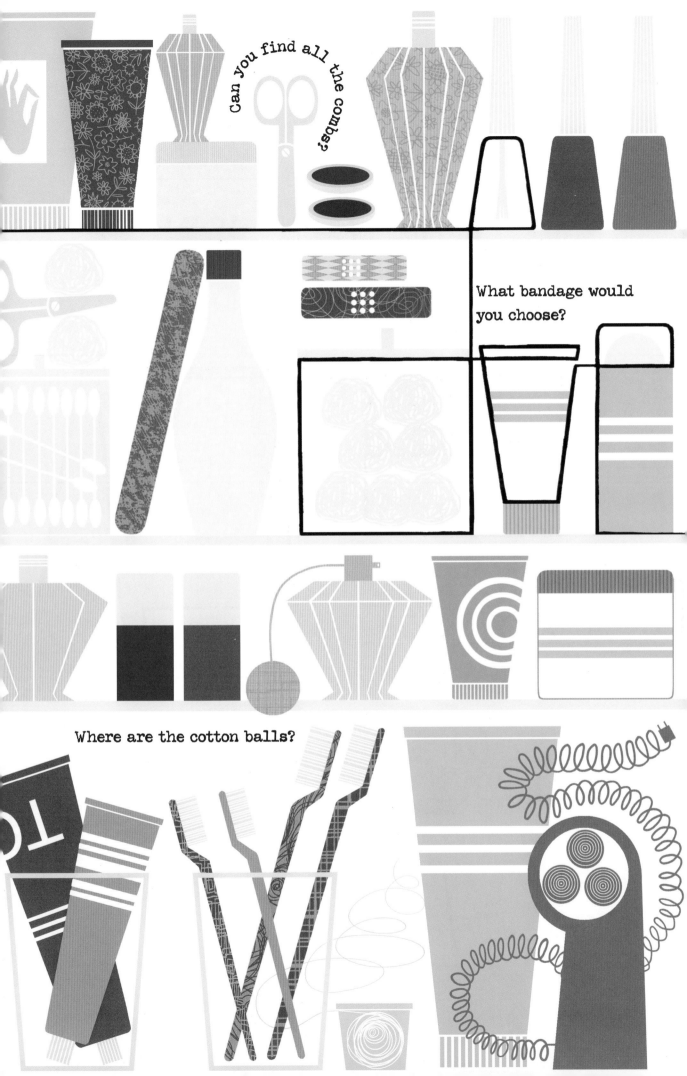

Can you find all the combs?

What bandage would you choose?

Where are the cotton balls?

Turn the page to find your
favorite toy in . . .

the toy box.

What are the colors on the xylophone?

Which letters are on the blocks?

Where are the toy cars and boats?

Can you find all the jigsaw puzzle pieces?

U Y T B E C K N S A R

How many cups are in the tea set?

What would you play with at the beach?

Now let's climb
up to the attic.

Turn the
page to find
what's hidden in . . .

the treasure chest.

243

What would you use to tell time?

How many photos are there?

What color is the record player?

579

BREV-KORT
CARTE POSTALE

Which medal has a bicycle on it?

How many keys do you see?

How many stars can you count?

1953

You followed the line all through the house.

As you were exploring,
did you see a mouse?

A few things were put
in spots that were wrong.

Where do those things really belong?